The Rat and the Tiger

Keiko Kasza

G. P. Putnam's Sons   New York

G. P. Putnam's Sons, a division of The Putnam & Grosset Group,
200 Madison Avenue, New York, NY 10016.
Published simultaneously in Canada.
Printed in Hong Kong by South China Printing Co. (1988) Ltd
Designed by Nanette Stevenson and Colleen Flis.
Library of Congress Cataloging-in-Publication Data
Kasza, Keiko.   The rat and the tiger/Keiko Kasza.   p.   cm.
Summary: In his friendship with Rat, Tiger takes
advantage and plays the bully because of his greater
size, but one day Rat stands up for his rights.
[1. Rats—Fiction. 2 Tigers—Fiction. 3. Friendship—Fiction.
4. Bullies—Fiction.] I. Title. PZ7.K15645Rat 1993 [E]—dc20 91-34413 CIP
ISBN 0-399-22404-1
1 3 5 7 9 10 8 6 4 2
First Impression

To my parents

I'm a rat, just a tiny little rat.
Tiger is a big tough fellow.
We are best friends.
   We used to have a little problem, though. . . .

Whenever we played cowboys,
Tiger was always the good guy,
and I was the bad guy.

Tiger said, "The good guy always wins in the end."
What could I say? I'm just a tiny little rat.

Whenever Tiger and I shared a doughnut, Tiger always
cut it so that his piece was bigger than mine.

Tiger said, "It's nice to share, isn't it?"
What could I say? I'm just a tiny little rat.

Whenever Tiger saw a flower he liked,
he just pointed and expected me
to get it for him.

Tiger said, "Isn't nature beautiful?"
What could I say? I'm just a tiny little rat.

One day I built a castle, the biggest one
I had ever made.
"Look, Tiger!" I shouted proudly.
Tiger said, "Nice job, Rat."

Then he jumped into the air and kicked
my castle to pieces!

"That's it, Tiger!" I screamed.
"You're not my friend anymore.
I may be a tiny little rat
but you're a big mean bully!
Good-bye!"

I was mad. And I was sad.
But most of all, I was scared.
I had never yelled at Tiger like that before.

When Tiger found me, my heart almost stopped. I thought he might kick me just like he had kicked my castle.

"Go away, Tiger!" I shouted.
"I'm not afraid of you. Leave me alone!"

But Tiger didn't come to kick me.
He had fixed my castle, and he
wanted me to see it. So I did.
  But I told him, "I'm still not
your friend."

Then Tiger asked me if I wanted to play the good cowboy for a change. So I did.

But I told him, "I'm still not your friend."

Next, Tiger asked me if I wanted to cut our doughnut for once.
So I did.

But I told him, "I'm still not your friend."

Finally, Tiger asked me if I wanted a flower.
So I pointed to one, and Tiger bravely
went to pick it for me.

"Maybe," I told him, "just maybe I'll be your friend again."
Tiger smiled.

Ever since that day, we have gotten along just fine. We take turns at everything. And we split our doughnuts right down the middle.

We do have a little problem, though. . . .

A new kid on the block!